Please return this book on or before the date shown above. To renew go to www.essex.gov.uk/libraries, ring 0845 603 7628 or go to any Essex library.

Essex County Council

Sue Graves

W

Essex County Council

3013020158001 5

First published in 2011 by
Franklin Watts
338 Euston Road
London NW1 3BH

Franklin Watts Australia
Level 17/207 Kent Street
Sydney NSW 2000

Text and illustration © Franklin Watts 2011

The Espresso characters are originated and
designed by Claire Underwood and Pesky Ltd.

The Espresso characters are the property of
Espresso Education Ltd.

A CIP catalogue record for this book is
available from the British Library.

ISBN: 978 1 4451 0428 7 (hbk)
ISBN: 978 1 4451 0441 6 (pbk)

Illustrations by Artful Doodlers Ltd.
Art Director: Jonathan Hair
Series Editor: Jackie Hamley
Series Designer: Matthew Lilly

Printed in China

Franklin Watts is a division of
Hachette Children's Books,
an Hachette UK company.

www.hachette.co.uk

Level 1 50 words
Concentrating on CVC words plus and, the, to

Level 2 70 words
Concentrating on double letter sounds and new letter
sounds (ck, ff, ll, ss, j, v, w, x, y, z, zz) plus no, go, I

Level 3 100 words
Concentrating on new graphemes (qu, ch, sh, th, ng,
ai, ee, igh, oa, oo, ar, or, ur, ow, oi, ear, air, ure, er)
plus he, she, we, me, be, was, my, you, they, her, all

Level 4 150 words
Concentrating on adjacent consonants (CVCC/CCVC
words) plus said, so, have, like, some, come, were, there,
little, one, do, when, out, what

Kim had a bat
and a ball.

I will hit my ball. If you get it, you win.

Kim hit the ball.
Ash ran to get it.

But the ball hit Scrap.

Kim hit the ball hard.
Polly ran to get it.

But the ball hit Scrap!

You did not get the ball, Polly. I win!

Kim hit the ball
high up in the air.
They all ran
to get it.

The ball shot up and up.

15

Scrap shot up, too!

He got the ball.

Puzzles

Match the words that rhyme to the pictures!

card

all

ball

bee

hard

thigh

fall

tree

lard

tall

high

see

sigh

Answers

ball – all, fall, tall   **tree** – bee, see

hard – card, lard   **high** – thigh, sigh

Espresso Connections

This book may be used in conjunction with the Literacy area on Espresso to secure children's phonics learning. Here are some suggestions.

Word Machine
Encourage children to play the Word Machine Level 1. Demonstrate how the machine works, and then move on to the activities.

Ask children to find the correct first letter. Then ask children to find the correct last letter. Then ask children to find the correct middle letter.

Check that children are able to hear the difference between the letter sounds as different words come up.

Praise plausible attempts, such as substituting the letter "k" for "c" when attempting to find the hard c sound.

Finally, ask children to find all the letters of the word.

Spot the Word
Load a big book, for example **"An unusual friendship"** to play Spot the Word.

Give children pieces of paper with the high frequency words he or they or all. (The class could be split, with groups of children looking for different words.)

Ask children to note down on the paper each time they have seen or heard the word they are looking for.

At the end of the book, children should count up how many times their target word has been used. If their word has not been used, where could it be used?

Go back through the book together and see whether they got it right.

Praise plausible attempts, for example "her" for "he" and take the opportunity to point out why these words are different.

You could replicate the activity with this phonics story.